Do these activities to prepare your child to read this book.

See It, Say It

Ask your child to color the star beside the word when he or she finds it in the book.

Make sure your child understands what each word means.

⭐ miracle   ⭐ finger

⭐ doctor   ⭐ squeeze

Does It Fit?

Help your child read these words out loud.

Then say, *Some of these words have the same sound at the beginning. Cross out three words that have a different beginning sound.*

blind	grapes	buy
sqeeze	bump	legs

To, With, and By

To	Read four pages out loud *to* your child. Run your finger under the words as you say them at a normal speed. Make sure your child is looking at the words.
With	Read the same four pages out loud *with* your child. Run your finger under the words as you say them at a normal speed. Your child will probably say every other word correctly.
By	Run your finger under the words as your child says them *by* himself or herself. Help your child fix any mistakes.

Continue doing *To, With, and By* a few pages at a time for the rest of this book. Have your child reread this story for the next several days until it sounds great and is practically memorized.

 Go to www.RocketReaders.com for more reading tips.

Faith Kidz® is an imprint of Cook Communications Ministries
Colorado Springs, Colorado 80918
Cook Communications, Paris, Ontario
Kingsway Communications,
Eastbourne, England

HOW DID THAT HAPPEN?
©2003 by Cook Communications

First printing, 2003
Printed in Korea
1 2 3 4 5 6 7 Printing/Year 07 06 05 04 03

Senior Editor: Heather Gemmen
Design Manager: Jeffrey P. Barnes
Designer: Kelly Robinson

How Did That Happen?

Rocket Readers Level 4

Written by
Heather Gemmen
and
Mary McNeil

Illustrated by
Dan Foote

Chapter 1

John 2:1–11

That was water.
Now it's wine.
How did that happen?

Did you snap your fingers?
Did you wave a wand?

Did you squeeze more grapes?
Did you run to the store?

I didn't snap my fingers.
I didn't squeeze more grapes.
I didn't do anything.

Jesus did a miracle!

Chapter 2

Mark 2:1–7

You couldn't walk.
Now you can!
How did that happen?

Did you exercise?
Did you read a book?

Did you make a wish?
Did you say the magic word?

What did you do?

Did you buy new legs?
Did you see a doctor?

I didn't make a wish.
I didn't buy new legs.
I didn't exercise.
I didn't do anything.

Jesus did a miracle!

Chapter 3

Matthew 15:29–31

You were blind.
Now you see!
How did that happen?

Did you bump your head?
Did you rub your eyes?

How did you do that?

Did you buy new eyes?
Did you see a doctor?

Did you make a wish?
Did you say the magic word?

I didn't make a wish.
I didn't buy new eyes.
I didn't bump my head.
I didn't do anything.

Jesus did a miracle!

Chapter 4

John 11:1–44

He was dead.
Now he is alive!
How did that happen?

Did you snap your fingers?
Did you wave a wand?

Did you ring a bell?
Did you sing a song?

I didn't snap my fingers.
I didn't ring a bell.
I didn't do anything.

Jesus did a miracle!

How Did That Happen?

Life Issue: I want my child to know that God can do anything.

Spiritual Building Block: Awe

Do the following activities to help your child grow in faith:

Sight: Invite your child to make a booklet that tells a story about something a person cannot do but God can do. This might include creating the world, a miraculous healing, or rising from the dead. Staple the pages together or punch holes and bind them together with yarn. On the front, add the title, "God Can Do Anything!"

Sound: Ask your child to give endings to these sentences:
Jesus changed water to _____.
Nothing is impossible with _____.
When I think about Jesus' miracles, I feel _____.

Touch: Have your child write these words from Mark 5:20 in the lines below.

All the people were amazed.